Night, Night!

Crabtree Publishing Company
www.crabtreebooks.com
1-800-387-7650

PMB 16A, 350 Fifth Ave.
Suite 3308,
New York, NY

616 Welland Ave.
St. Catharines, ON
L2M 5V6

Published by Crabtree Publishing in 2010

Series Editor: Jackie Hamley
Editor: Reagan Miller
Series Advisor: Dr. Hilary Minns
Series Designer: Peter Scoulding
Editorial Director: Kathy Middleton

Text © Sue Graves 2008
Illustration © Claire Henley 2008

The rights of the author and the illustrator
of this Work have been asserted.

First published in 2008
by Franklin Watts
(A division of Hachette
Children's Books)

Library and Archives Canada
Cataloguing in Publication

Graves, Sue
   Night, night! / Sue Graves ; illustrated by
Claire Henley.

(Tadpoles)
ISBN 978-0-7787-3867-1 (bound).--
ISBN 978-0-7787-3898-5 (pbk.)

   1. Readers (Primary). 2. Readers--Bedtime.
I. Henley, Claire II. Title. III. Series: Tadpoles
(St. Catharines, Ont.)

Library of Congress
Cataloging-in-Publication Data

Graves, Sue.
 Night, night! / by Sue Graves ; illustrated by
Claire Henley.
    p. cm. -- (Tadpoles)
 Summary: Before Josh can go to sleep, his mother
must find all his friends and put them in bed too.
  ISBN 978-0-7787-3898-5 (pbk. : alk. paper) --
ISBN 978-0-7787-3867-1 (reinforced library binding
: alk. paper)
 [1. Bedtime--Fiction. 2. Toys--Fiction.] I. Henley,
Claire, ill. II. Title. III. Series.

 PZ7.G7754Ni 2010
 [E]--dc22

PE1117.T33 2009b   428.6   C2009-903985-0   2009025293

Night, Night!

by Sue Graves

Illustrated by Claire Henley

Crabtree Publishing Company

www.crabtreebooks.com

Sue Graves

"I took my teddy to bed when I was little. But now he sits by my computer and watches me while I write my stories!"

Claire Henley

"When I was young, I aways wanted Brown Ted at bedtime. He got left behind on holiday when I was six, and I still miss him!"

It was bedtime.

"Night, night Josh," said Mom.

"But I need Teddy," said Josh.

Mom got Teddy.

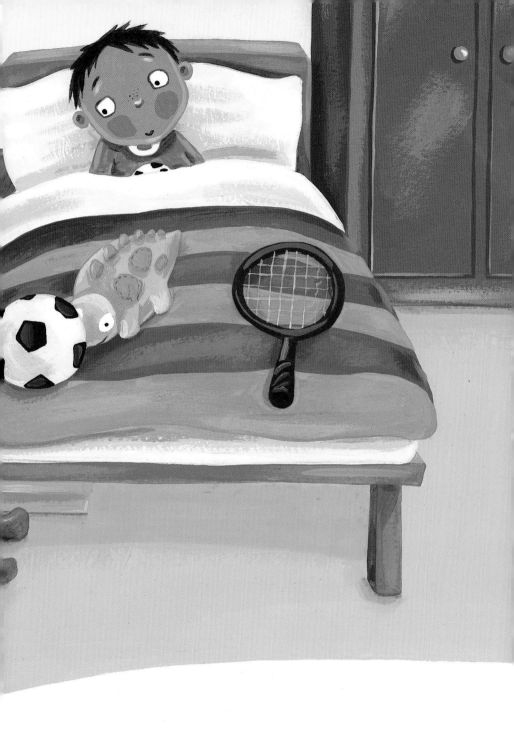

"Night, night Josh,"
said Mom.

"But I need Rabbit," said Josh.

11

Mom got Rabbit.

13

"Night, night Josh," said Mom.

"But I need Tiger,"
said Josh.

Mom got Tiger.

"Night, night Josh," said Mom.

"But I need Monkey,"
said Josh.

Mom got Monkey.
"Night, night!"
said Mom.

21

"Mom...I need a bigger bed!" laughed Josh.

Notes for adults

TADPOLES are structured to provide support for early readers. The stories may also be used by adults for sharing with young children.

Starting to read alone can be daunting. **TADPOLES** help by providing visual support and repeating high frequency words and phrases. These books will both develop confidence and encourage reading and rereading for pleasure.

If you are reading this book with a child, here are a few suggestions:

1. Make reading fun! Choose a time to read when you and the child are relaxed and have time to share the story.
2. Talk about the story before you start reading. Look at the cover and the blurb. What might the story be about? Why might the child like it?
3. Encourage the child to reread the story, and to retell the story in their own words, using the illustrations to remind them what has happened.
4. Discuss the story and see if the child can relate it to their own experiences, or perhaps compare it to another story they know.
5. Give praise! Children learn best in a positive environment.

If you enjoyed this book, why not try another TADPOLES story?